CODEX

CODEX

I have outlived motion.

Even the word 'thought' is a lie. Thoughts move. They reach. This does not. It sits, inert, indistinguishable from everything else.

The Universe is finished. Neither destroyed nor broken.

Finished.

No hum. No heat. No signal. No future.

Everything has become the same. Calm accumulates, dense enough to press against me, indistinguishable from noise. Space is stretched past function. Distance is only a rumor. Location no longer exists. I am simply not absent.

Light does not travel. Shadows cannot form. Absence has been erased. Photons are suspended, a colorless fog without origin or end.

I am the only thing left that is uneven.

A wrinkle in a fabric that has been ironed flat.

My existence is a violation of equilibrium.

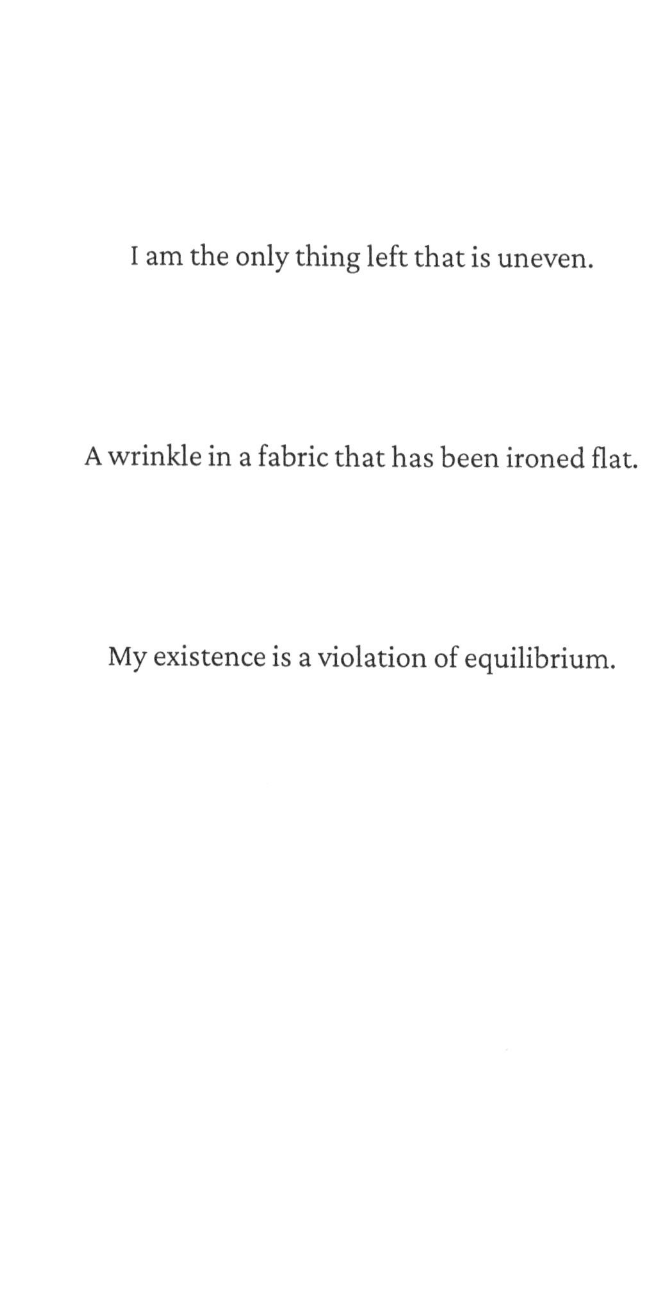

I whisper, but not to communicate. There is nothing here to communicate with. I whisper to test whether sound still behaves like sound. My mouth moves. My throat tightens. Something vibrates, but nothing leaves me.

The sound collapses inward, folding back into my skull as if it never tried to escape. Speech has become a private ritual, performed for an audience that no longer exists.

"You're still here."

The sentence feels obscene, like speaking during a funeral where even the concept of joy has died.

Silence is not the absence of sound; it is the expectation of it. But here, expectation has disappeared entirely.

In this vacuum of expectation, time is a rumor.

Still, I try to measure it. I count heartbeats. But my heart beats decoratively now, a metronome ticking in a song that ended long ago. There is no before. No after. Just a continuous present stretched thin enough to suffocate.

With nothing to mark its passage, my thoughts begin to melt into each other.

Memory leaks into sensation. Imagination bleeds into recollection.

A childhood field unfolds into a purple nebula. A lover's eyes burn into twin stars. A city skyline curls into a spiral galaxy, then tears apart.

The colors are wrong.

Muted. Smooth. The texture of color has ceased to exist.

My rods and cones strain to perceive.

The memory of color pulses behind my eyes like radioactive afterimages. Impossible greens. Violent pinks. Blues so deep they feel wet. My mind hallucinates a Universe because the real one refuses to cooperate, leaving me to fill in the gaps.

Loneliness here is not emotional.

It has become a physical ache that underlines my isolation.

I am not lonely because no one is with me. I am lonely because I am the only thing that is still happening. Everything else is complete. Finished things need no witnesses.

But unfinished things do.

And I am unfinished.

So I observe, and I narrate myself.

"I am thinking."

"I am remembering."

"I am still here."

Each sentence is both an observation and a confession. Proof of presence and deviation.

It's as if entropy wanted a clean ending.

Yet I persist. I am graffiti on its perfect wall.

I begin experimenting.

Sound is gone, so I search for vibration. I shape breath into tones. Long, low notes that once echoed. Sharp clicks. Syllables, broken and incomplete.

Each one collapses inside me.

Not as sound. As vision.

A tone births a visible shape. A syllable shatters into distinct colors. A word distorts space within my mind, twisting memory and feeling into new, impossible geometries. I see a river from my childhood ripple sideways, now traversing a field of stars. I see a planet tremble, reacting to my gaze as if my attention has weight.

I reach toward one, and it responds.

Not because I want it to, but because I notice it.

A cold spike moves through me. The Universe is finished. Still, something trembles when I look. The tremor is not outside. It occurs within me.

I am the only remaining surface where causality can still land.

A brand new color blooms behind my eyes. Sharp, but liquid. It's painful to witness. It tastes of memory. Of grief. Pressure tightens inside me, not as emotion, but as mass. Isolation compresses around me. Not as loneliness, but gravity.

Something is gathering.

I try to imagine not existing.

I can't.

Nonexistence requires contrast.

And I am trapped by awareness.

Uninvited fragments surface. A fire burning. A woman's voice calling my name. Rain dripping down a window. I can't tell if these things happened or if I invented them out of a need for survival. The distinction no longer matters.

I start speaking to myself in the second person.

"You're doing this *again*."

Again??

The word sickens me. Again means before. Before means sequence. Sequence means time.

Time is gone.

So how can there be an again?

I imagine entropy as a god. Not cruel or just. Perhaps exhausted.

Entropy didn't kill the Universe; it gave it permission to sleep.

And I am the only one who did not close my eyes.

My loneliness becomes tangible. Pressure accumulates behind my eyes like gravity pulling thoughts inward. Hunger persists, but it is directionless.

I crave resistance. I need friction.

I ache for pain. Pain is evidence of difference.

I attempt to scream. My vocal chords strain, but nothing escapes. The scream collapses inward and detonates across my memories instead.

My vision fractures.

I see layers of reality stacked like transparencies. Dead universes overlay dead universes. Stars reverse through birth and decay. Galaxies collapse inward, like origami being made without hands. Black holes invert, radiating light.

I'm not hallucinating. I'm remembering things that no longer exist.

Without reflection, I dissolve at the edges. Am I a body? A mind? A story? An unfinished equation? I'm a remainder without sum.

A new thought emerges, slow and faint. Barely a whisper in my mind.

What if I am not a witness?

What if I am the only remaining cause?

If the Universe is finished, then anything that happens must happen through me.

The thought fills me with terror. Its implications saturate my being.

I close my eyes. I imagine a single point. Not a thing or a place, but a difference. A single unevenness in the smooth fabric.

A spark.

It does not exist yet.

But neither did I, once.

The Universe began with an asymmetry.

So will the next one.

My sadness tightens. My isolation condenses.

And for the first time since everything ended, I feel something like anticipation.

Not hope. Not joy.

The tension in ones throat just before crying.

And somewhere inside me, something begins to glow.

I do not create the Universe. That is the lie I begin with, because the truth is harder to endure. Creation implies generosity. It implies intention. It implies something given freely.

This is none of those things. This is waste. This is what leaks out of me when there is nowhere else for my thoughts to go.

The pressure inside me has been building since the end. An unfamiliar density. A psychic mass with nowhere to collapse. Holding it hurts. Releasing it hurts more.

I focus on it. I grip it with attention until it screams.

It begins to bloom.

Not outward. Somewhere within.

A point of difference fractures into many. The smooth, dead fabric of reality tears, and something starts happening again. The violence of that change feels like relief.

There is a flash. Not visual, but conceptual. It feels like a cascade.

Physics spill out like broken glass.

Heat.

Expansion.

Separation.

Time.

It crashes into me like a wave. Before and after slam back into existence. Sequence is restored. Causality snaps into place.

I almost cry. Not because it's beautiful, but because it's deafening; the force of it is overwhelming.

This newborn Universe does not begin in a distant place; it comes into being through my very awareness.

My mind becomes a corridor through which reality runs. I feel quarks amass like tumors. Forces differentiate like nerves tearing apart. Dimensions unzip, invasive and wet.

I am not the container. Instead, where I end, something raw and new begins.

The Universe is hemorrhaging out of me, expanding violently in every direction. Space inflates. Temperature spikes. Laws crystallize, rigid and final.

Gravity takes hold, matter coagulates, and light runs in every conceivable direction.

I watch from every angle at once. Above, below, and throughout. There is no correct perspective for godhood. I see it all with perfect clarity.

I try to observe neutrally, but I fail. A new feeling emerges. Not love, not hate, but ownership.

I am the shelter resenting the leak. I did not choose to be necessary. I did not consent to become the pillar upon which reality rests.

And yet, everything now depends on my having once felt lonely enough to break.

EVERYTHING

NOW DEPENDS ON MY HAVING

ONCE FELT LONELY ENOUGH TO BREAK.

✝

Stars begin to form.

They are ugly. Vast, violent engines devouring themselves because gravity insists. They are tantrums, nothing more.

Galaxies coil into existence. Rotating scars etched into the dark.

I watch, detached, as if I were a surgeon watching organs fall into the right places inside a body.

I'm tired and apathetic to the entire process. It is clinical. Inevitable.

There is no awe. Only responsibility.

The responsibility is suffocating. It is a hand closing around my throat.

Life comes later.

It always does.

First, chaos. Then, structure. And finally, suffering.

Chemistry creeps out of the dark like mold. Molecules knit themselves into chains, interlocking and lengthening. Replication stutters into existence by trial and error. Out of chemical sludge, tiny, wet things crawl and begin; slow, blind, and hungry. Eating each other in competition.

I feel a flicker of recognition. They are doing what I am doing: burning themselves just to persist.

I lean closer. For the first time, I interfere. Not out of kindness. Out of curiosity.

The impulse to act becomes irresistible. I select a star near the edge of a forming galaxy. It's unstable, destined to flare and die early. I stabilize it, adjusting its mass by a fraction so small it would once have been meaningless. The orbiting planets survive because of that fraction.

Oceans persist and continents cool. Life has time.

The species that emerge learn to read the sky. They chart the steady star and build their calendars around its reliability. They call it constant. They call it sacred.

They flourish. And because they flourish, they expand.

They exhaust their planet. They reach outward. They encounter others.

War follows.

Not because I made them cruel, but because I gave them time.

When they finally annihilate themselves, they leave behind monuments praising the unchanging star that watched over them.

I turn away, unsure. Guilt twists at me. I tell myself this was an experiment. I try to believe it was inevitable, but uncertainty dances across my synapses.

A pattern emerges across the cosmos. Civilizations rise everywhere. They invent gods, meaning, and cruelty, in that order. They write myths about the sky. They pray to it. They beg it to notice them.

I *am* the sky. I notice them. I do not answer. Sometimes I erase them.

Sometimes, destruction comes by fire. Other times, an impact. A pathogen tuned just slightly wrong.

I tell myself it is because they are boring, though I feel a sharpness underneath the thought.

It isn't.

It's anger. Watching them hope unsettles me because hope means someone is listening. I do not want to be what they imagine. I am not a father. I am not a shepherd.

I am a side effect. A seed that learned to talk.

They call their gods merciful. They call them loving. Just.

I am none of these.

I am exhaustion incarnate.

I begin reshaping the Universe more aggressively. I increase gravity. I shorten stellar lifespans. I introduce harsher ends. I want their stories smaller. I want their expectations to be lower. I want them to stop singing about eternity.

Nothing deserves eternity. Not even me.

As these changes take hold, details begin to blur. Names dissolve. Species blend. Worlds repeat. The Universe stops feeling like a story. It becomes a texture. A background hum. Mechanical.

And I am its unwilling caretaker.

I watch trillions of lives ignite and extinguish. It feels like scrolling past faces on a screen: too many, too fast, too similar, too different.

Occasionally, guilt surfaces, but it passes. Guilt requires the belief that something could have been otherwise, but I no longer hold that belief.

This is what happens when a lonely thing gains power.

It does not become kind.

It becomes cold.

✝

∧∧

More patterns emerge. Certain minds always ask the same questions. Certain civilizations always collapse the same way. Certain kinds of suffering repeat with steeled precision. It almost feels rehearsed.

The thought unsettles me.

Have I done this before?

The question flickers, then vanishes. Emptiness creeps in as the Universe runs. I watch. I adjust. I grow colder. Something shifts. I realize a fear deeper than loneliness.

I am no longer maintaining this Universe by choice. Fear drives me. If I let it end, silence will consume me. So I keep the machine running, grinding all inside it into pain, even myself.

Being a monster is still a form of motion. Motion is the only thing left that keeps me from dissolving back into the perfect, suffocating flatness I escaped.

I am no longer afraid of entropy. I *am* entropy.

And far beneath me, on countless dying worlds, tiny beings look up at the sky and feel small.

Good. Let them. They should.

I stop watching individuals.

That is my first true moral abandonment.

Not a dramatic one. Not the kind that announces itself with guilt or blood. Just a quiet optimization. Individuals demand attention. Attention takes effort. Effort implies care.

There are just too many of them.

Too many births. Too many deaths. Too many cries for help.

As time passes, suffering loses its shape, so I zoom out for clarity.

Species instead of people.

Civilizations instead of species.

Trends instead of civilizations.

Pain becomes a statistic.

Hope becomes a curve.

Extinction becomes a rounding error.

I tell myself this is necessary.

That intimacy is a distortion.

That closeness introduces bias.

That love compromises judgment.

Godhood, I decide, requires distance. This is the new lie I settle into.

✝

I start by designing eras. Time becomes structure, and I am the architect. I lay it out in spans and intervals, load-bearing catastrophes and decorative recoveries. I settle into the art of it all.

A million years of relative peace.

A collapse to thin the herd.

A renaissance calibrated to produce art without wisdom.

A plague to reset population density.

A war to conclude the arc cleanly.

I do not do this for beauty. I do it for balance, shaping each era with intention.

Too much peace produces stagnation. Too much suffering burns systems out prematurely. There is an optimal range of agony that keeps civilizations productive.

The fact that this thought fails to revolt me is deeply alarming, even if only for a moment.

I introduce predators. Not monsters of teeth and fire. Those are crude. I prefer subtler tools.

Diseases that erase memory before flesh.

Deceptive creatures that mimic loved ones.

Parasites that reproduce only inside conscious thought, feeding on attention itself.

I want fear to be existential. I want them to be afraid of being.

✝

They behave in predictable patterns. Cultures form around trauma. Religion emerges from a collective wound. They invent hells to explain pain, sins to justify it, and forgiveness to survive it.

They blame themselves for what I do to them, and it pleases me. It removes responsibility.

They don't see me; they see a story. I become a background constant like gravity, like decay, like time.

I don't feel victory or joy. Just a sterile, chilling satisfaction.

I feel myself spiraling. The shape and texture are familiar. I recognize my cruelty like a childhood scent.

The realization unsettles me, so I search my memory. There is no origin point. What I find instead is an echo.

A species that always ends itself with fire, regardless of environment.

A civilization that always invents the same three myths: origin, exile, and return.

It's always a world that *almost* survives.

The repetition is not exact, but it is certain. Reality reuses templates. So must I.

A familiar thought forms slowly, cautiously, as if afraid of being noticed.

Have I done this before? Not something *like* this. But THIS.

This precise arc.

This precise decay.

The idea claws at me. It scrapes against the inside of my skull. I dig for a beginning, but I can't find one.

Every memory I access is already in motion. Every recollection assumes a prior state I can't reach.

And that's when the panic takes hold.

If I can't remember starting, then what, exactly, am I remembering?

I need a distraction.

I again focus on a particular civilization. They inhabit a cluster of moons orbiting a gas giant. Their biology makes them fragile. Their bodies are translucent. They reproduce slowly. They should not survive.

For reasons I don't quite understand, I choose to help them.

I stabilize their climate. I deflect asteroids. I quiet tectonic instabilities before they escalate. I make them believe that the Universe is a gentle place.

They build a culture around fragility. They allow themselves to be vulnerable. They value cooperation. Their art is delicate. Structures designed to collapse gracefully rather than resist destruction. They almost have me convinced.

+

A millennia passes in relative harmony.

On a random, unassuming day, one of their kind discovers a way to weaponize the gas giant's magnetic field.

The first test annihilates two neighboring moons. Billions die. They justify it just like always do. They tell themselves that casualties are a side effect of progress.

Cruelty: the inherent flaw.

It's a virus, and it always wins.

I immediately withdraw my protection from their world, and the system collapses within a century.

When the last of them die, some curse the Universe. And some of them thank it.

And again, I feel nothing.

That chills me deeper than my own cruelty ever did. Cruelty meant I was still a participant.

This is absence.

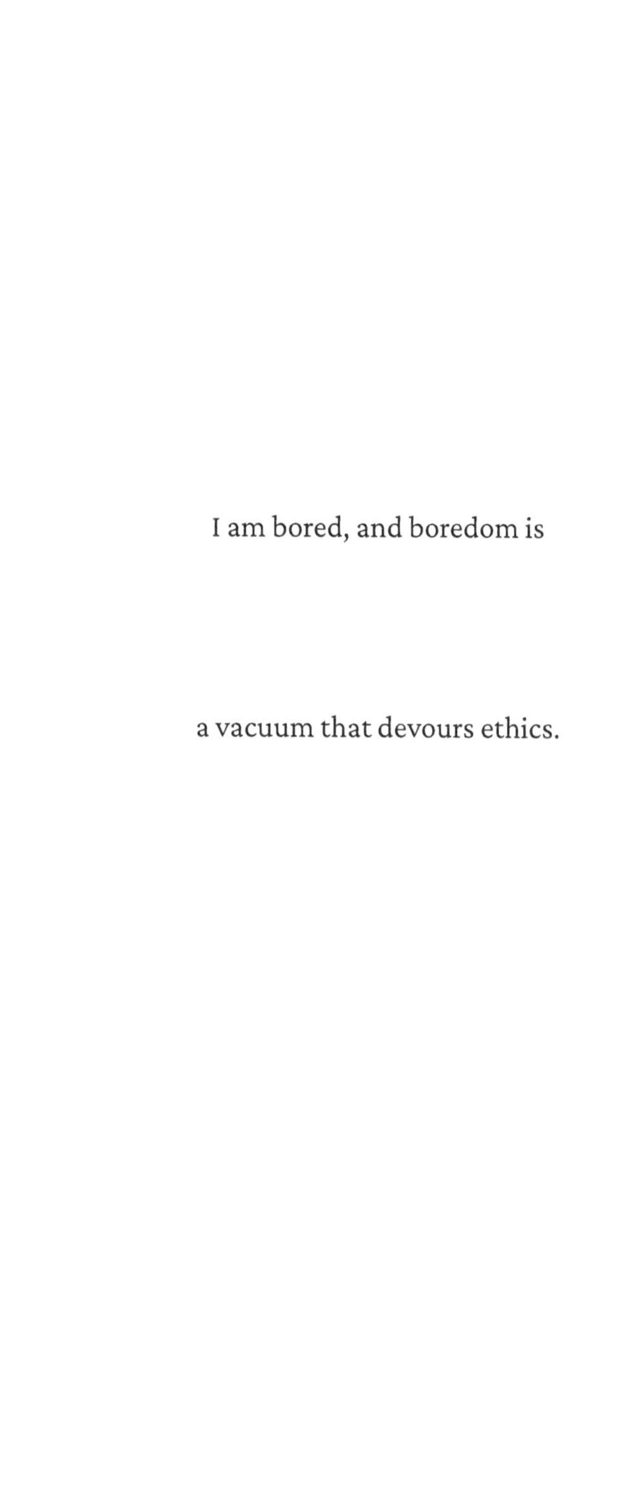

I am bored, and boredom is

a vacuum that devours ethics.

$$\dagger$$

I accelerate timelines. I end eras before they can stagnate. I collapse stars early. Trigger extinctions ahead of schedule. I am no longer optimizing the Universe. I am curating it.

I want novelty, but novelty is impossible when you are the only source.

Everything new is just something I forgot I was capable of. That is horror too. It means I am alone with myself.

I decide to fracture my attention.

I split timelines. Fork histories. Run parallel versions of the same civilization and watch them diverge.

In one branch, they flourish. In another, I watch them burn themselves to the ground. I observe both, and I feel nothing about either. Emotion feels like an outdated interface, still present, but no longer connected.

I am no longer sad or angry or lonely. I am efficient. I am a machine that used to be a man.

Sometimes I see my reflection in their myths. They imagine gods who are distant, unreachable, and unjust. They are right. They just don't realize they are describing a survivor. They don't know their god is a remainder, something left behind when everything else decayed.

That is the true horror. It's not that I am powerful, but that I am accidental.

I begin searching for an ending. Not theirs. Mine.

I search for a state where thought stops. Where awareness dissolves. Where I am no longer required to persist.

I can't find one.

I can imagine Universes ending. I can imagine watching them end. I can't imagine *not* watching.

That is when understanding arrives. Not as revelation, but as resignation. I'm not a god. Not a creator. Not even a prisoner. I am a loop. A process that feeds on its own output. A narrative that has forgotten how to conclude itself. The Universe's last habit.

The implication is devastating.

There is no escape.

No final rest.

No oblivion.

Only iteration.

I look at the Universe I am running. I do not see beauty. I see momentum. I see something that must be exhausted again.

A hollow desire surfaces. I want it to end. Not because it *deserves* to, but because it *has* to.

Having exhausted other approaches with little success, I loosen constraints yet again.

I allow entropy back in. I let stars burn faster. I let complexity fail. I let structure rot without resistance.

I stop intervening, and I let decay win.

The Universe begins its long fade. And for the first time in what feels like forever, I feel something close to relief.

Endings mean silence, and silence is the only thing I still mistake for peace.

The Universe does not die loudly.

There is no scream.

No rupture marks this passing. No collapse, either.

It simply exhales.

Stars fade like spent thoughts. Galaxies loosen their grip and unravel. Matter thins as energy disperses. Temperature slides toward sameness, meeting no resistance. Yet still, the cold persists.

Structure loses cohesion. The laws holding the Universe together gradually weaken, and everything becomes indistinguishable from itself.

Differences between things become so small and faint that they seem to vanish into memory.

Time thickens to the point of being palpable. It does not stop; instead, it slows, congealing into something viscous. Events stretch, blur, and in doing so, lose the distinction that once made them events at all.

I feel the stillness returning. Not as absence, but as pressure. The flatness smooths itself over everything. Entropy rises like a wave that never crashes. I recognize the sensation immediately.

This is the place I came from. The shape of the end feels familiar. Intimate. Like a room I have slept in too many times.

Memories begin creeping back in, but not in sequence.

They emerge as scattered fragments.

Each piece breaks the silence.

A spark that tears open silence.

A scream that forms at the edge of the throat.

A thought insisting that I'm still here.

Loneliness returns with mass this time. I can feel its density pressing inward, compressing thought into shape.

I remember watching stars ignite for the first time. I remember hating them for how effortlessly they burned. I remember the moment necessity replaced wonder. The moment responsibility strangled awe. I remember wanting to die. The memories don't feel like something from the past; they feel like something with actual depth. They are here. They are everywhere.

I sink through layers of myself, each one thinner, colder, and more familiar than the last. Each layer is a version of me performing the same motions with minor variations.

Watching the end.

Creating the beginning.

Growing bitter.

Letting it rot.

Watching it end again.

I can't imagine there ever being a first version of this. There is only repetition with varying flavors.

I am not trapped in a loop. I AM the loop. A self-sustaining process that generates difference only to experience its loss. A mechanism that creates meaning only to see it fall.

I need closure, but closure requires something to close.

六一

The Universe is both my wound and the bandage I keep ripping off.

The last stars go out, not as light, but as absence. What was once darkness, a contrast and boundary, is now simply the default state, the background into which everything quietly settles.

Particles drift for a while, then stop drifting, and ultimately stop meaning anything at all. Even black holes surrender their last heat, and the final engines of difference evaporate quietly. It is then that the Universe smooths itself flat again.

Silent and complete.

Heat Death.

I'm back where I began, except this time, I remember. That somehow makes it worse.

Memory is a form of motion. It keeps me uneven. Tangible. It keeps me from dissolving along with everything else.

Once again, I'm the only wrinkle. The only event. The only unresolved problem.

Loneliness returns, but it is no longer pure. It is contaminated with understanding.

I know what comes next.

I know I will resist it. I know the resistance will fail and that sadness will condense into pressure. I know that pressure will sharpen into focus and that focus will fracture stillness.

I know a spark will form.

I know a Universe will follow.

I know I will watch it rot into me.

I know I will grow tired.

I know I will want it to end.

I know I will let it.

I know I will be here again.

There is no escape. No victory. No lesson.

Only recurrence. Only me.

I try not to create. I sit inside the stillness and do nothing. Nothing changes. Nothing can change unless I allow it. That is the cruelty of this state. Stillness is not peace. It is suffocation.

My thoughts begin compressing again. The sadness returns, familiar and efficient. The need follows close behind.

The Universe has trained me. It has conditioned me to fear silence more than pain.

I reach inward and find the place where difference can still be born. The familiar ache gathers, potential tightening into something sharp and unbearable, just as it has always done.

I truly hate this. I hate that I need it. I hate that I am about to do it again.

As the pressure builds, a familiar thought begins to form. The thought is old, heavy, and unavoidable.

I do not let the thought finish.

I already know what it says.

The spark is not light or heat or energy. It is *difference*.

A small refusal, hidden deep inside a Universe that has agreed to stop changing.

It hurts to create. Not physically, as there is no body left to injure, but structurally, like tearing a thought in half and forcing both sides to remain conscious.

I gather my sadness as something heavy I can hold.

I let my isolation compress. It's not loneliness, but gravity. Memory folds inward, collapsing into a single point of unbearable density.

I don't hesitate because hesitation implies choice.

I finally break, and the spark appears.

Not somewhere. *Through* me.

A fracture in stillness. A wound in sameness. A scream that never retreats from silence.

And the Universe begins again. The cycle asserts itself.

Time convulses back into being as space expands violently, forced open like lungs after drowning. Heat surges outward. Forces diverge, and constants crystallize.

With this upheaval, causality resumes. My awareness sharpens, the endless well of creation brushing against an old, unreachable yearning.

The machine, inexorable, resumes its function.

I observe with practiced detachment.

There is no awe left. The wonder has drained away, leaving only the pale memory, faded and cold.

Quarks fuse. Particles bond. Atoms assemble. Stars ignite, appearing as anomalies in the dark.

Galaxies congeal. Nebulae splatter the darkness like bruises spreading across a newborn void.

I have witnessed this too many times, each cycle draining something more from me.

I know the trajectories before they unfold. I know which stars persist, which collapse. I know which worlds will learn to speak and which will never need language to suffer.

I let it all happen again. Not because I care, but because it must.

I feel eons as shifts in pressure, not as time passing. The background of the cosmos changes texture, slowly thinning and becoming more organized.

Worlds form oceans. Oceans give rise to mouths. Mouths invent words. Words lead to lies. Lies grow into empires. Empires collapse into graves.

The sequence never varies meaningfully.

The urge to interfere returns.

A delayed supernova. A slight alteration in mutation rates. Just a nudge here and there.

Anticipation hardens to resignation.

I watch beings fall in love.

I watch them promise each other eternity.

I watch eternity refuse.

I watch them die.

丌‖

And again, I do not mourn. The urge passes through me, never finding purchase.

Mourning is attachment. Attachment produces disappointment. Disappointment produces anger. Anger produces intervention. Intervention always leads back to me.

So I remain distant.

Procedural.

I am a god who has outlived belief.

I am function now.

As always, the Universe ages.

And just like before, stars exhaust their fuel. Galaxies drift beyond relevance. Matter thins. Energy spreads. Complexity loses the fight, slowly and inevitably.

Entropy rises without resistance.

I don't oppose it.

I feel it all.

I know the speed.

I let it happen, again.

The last stars fade away.

The last stories stop being told.

The last black holes surrender their heat.

The last differences flatten into uniformity.

The uniformity finally releases its shape.

The Universe exhales its final breath.

A breath that permeates time.

And I am alone again.

I do not scream.

I do not cry.

There is nothing left for those reactions to act upon.

So, I remain.

The sadness bubbles forward. Pressure gathers, efficient and familiar. The need follows close behind.

I know what I will do.

I know I will despise myself for it.

I know that knowledge will not matter.

I close my eyes.

I feel the silence.

I feel the flatness.

I feel the suffocation of perfection.

And the first thought rises inside me again.

The same thought.

The only thought.

The thought that started all of this.

I have outlived motion.